The Forest of Forgotten Names
By B. Humphrey

Dedicated with love to Kyleigh, Jordan, Littleface and Ears McEarson

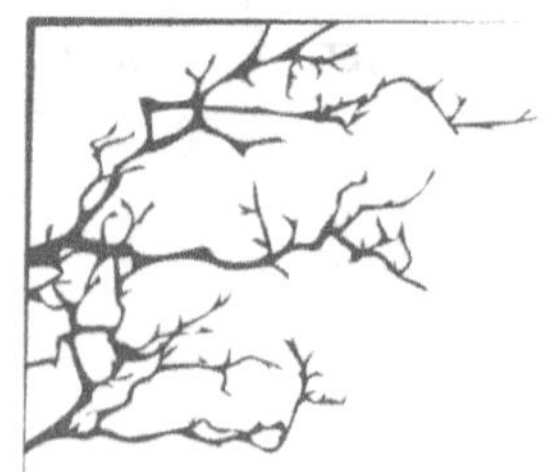

Prologue

In a forest far from the heavy footprints of men, there is a secret—a garden no map can chart and no path leads to. It hides beneath a canopy stitched from threads of amber and gold, where every leaf glimmers like a whispered memory waiting to be remembered. To stumble upon this place, you cannot simply look; you must have lost something, something precious enough to leave an ache behind. Only then will the garden's gate unlock, and the forest will know you by name.

On this particular autumn evening, the world exhaled, and the forest drank in the crispness of twilight. **The air tasted of ripe apples and woodsmoke**, a lingering sweetness drifting through brambles and briars. Leaves tumbled lazily, drifting like little paper boats set afloat on invisible rivers. Somewhere in the high boughs of a maple, a squirrel scolded the wind for chasing away the last of the acorns, while below, a fox's burrow glowed warmly from within, a lantern casting long shadows across the earth.

The forest was **alive with murmurs and quiet mischief**. A moth danced between rays of dimming sunlight. The creek whispered stories to the stones beneath it. And the wind—a trickster tonight—plucked a branch here, rattled a window there, as if daring the world to listen closely.

But, as magical as the forest was, there was a sadness in the roots and branches, a thinning of magic that drifted through like the first signs of winter's chill. **The human world was forgetting**—forgetting the old stories, the names carved into the bark of ancient trees, the songs whispered to the stars. And when magic is forgotten, it withers like a flower pressed too long between the pages of a book.

Still, **hope stirred among the shadows**. For tonight, the forest whispered a name it hadn't spoken in many, many years—Willa.

Somewhere on the edge of the forest, not too far from the last streetlight and just beyond the reach of the city's noise, **a girl with wild, wind-tangled hair** stood beneath a heavy oak tree. **Her fingers worried the string of an acorn necklace**—a little treasure from her grandmother—and tonight, for the first time, she noticed it was missing.

The knot in her chest grew tight, a small ache blooming there, as if losing the acorn had somehow lost something more—a memory she couldn't quite grasp. **A breeze curled around her, carrying with it the scent of pine and cinnamon, coaxing her forward, deeper into the trees.** She didn't think twice. There was nothing waiting for her at home but empty rooms and unanswered questions. So, she let her feet move without direction, following the scent of autumn, as if some invisible hand had taken hers.

The forest opened before her like a storybook—a hush settling over the world as if the trees leaned in, curious about this new visitor. **Golden leaves carpeted the ground, and the light slipped through branches in ribbons**, wrapping Willa in their glow. The farther she went, the quieter it became, until the only sound was the soft crunch of her steps and the far-off chatter of squirrels planning their winter hoards.

And then—just as the wind sighed through the treetops—**she saw it something.** At first, it was only a flicker: **a glimpse of shimmering light, like moonlight caught in a spider's web.** But as Willa stepped closer, the air itself seemed to shift—**warmer, richer**, as though she had wandered into a dream. The garden revealed itself slowly, like an old friend smiling after years apart. **A stone arch draped in ivy**, twinkling with morning dew, stood before her, as if saying: *Here you are. We've been waiting.*

Willa blinked, her breath a puff of white in the cooling air. For a moment, it felt as if **the trees were holding their breath**, watching her, waiting to see if she'd step through. And something inside her stirred—a quiet knowing, as if she belonged here, even though she'd never been.

She reached out, her hand brushing the ivy, and as she did, the stones beneath the arch shimmered with a faint hum, like the strings of a harp plucked by unseen hands. **A voice—soft, like the rustle of leaves—whispered somewhere above her:**

"Names are not so easily lost, little one. They wait for you, right where you left them."

With a deep breath, Willa stepped through the arch, and the world on the other side unfolded before her—a place made of forgotten things and lingering magic. The kind of place where stories slept under every stone and dreams grew like wildflowers in the cracks.

And thus, her journey began. A journey that would lead her to **a mischievous fairy named Larkspur, a treehouse witch** called **Bramble**, and **a burrowing fox named Mr. Tawnycoat**, all of whom knew the secret to restoring what had been lost.

But time was running out, and **the first frost would come soon, chasing away the last of the golden leaves**. If the garden was to survive, Willa would have to remember what the rest of the world had forgotten.

Because some things—names, stories, and magic—are only ever lost if we stop believing in them. And sometimes, all it takes to bring them back is a little girl with an open heart and a missing acorn necklace.

And so, the forest whispered on...

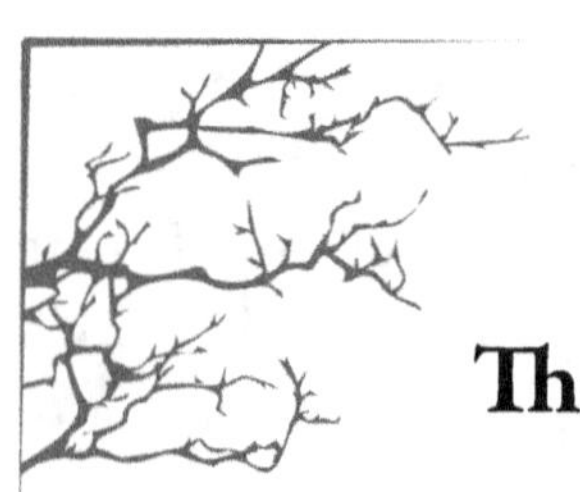

The Lost Name

The morning sun had barely stretched its golden arms when **Willa Jacobs** wandered deeper into the forest, each step stirring fallen leaves into playful dances around her boots. **The woods greeted her like an old friend**—branches arching overhead in a grand cathedral of gold, crimson, and ochre. A cool breeze kissed her cheeks, carrying the scents of cinnamon, pine, and a distant promise of winter's frost. She pulled her jacket tight, though the chill did not bother her. Something else tugged at her heart, as soft and insistent as the wind: **the absence of her acorn necklace**.

It wasn't just a necklace. It was a story—one woven between Willa and her grandmother, a reminder of afternoons spent under the oak tree where her grandmother whispered old tales into her ear. Stories about lost things finding their way back, about magic waiting in hidden places. And now, that little acorn, smooth and warm from countless touches, was gone. **The ache in her chest deepened, and with it came a quiet sense of urgency.**

"Go to the forest," her grandmother once said. *"The trees will know what you've lost, even when you don't."*

So she did. Willa walked until the ground sloped away beneath her feet, her breath fogging in the brisk autumn air. She followed no trail, but something—**an unseen thread of longing**—drew her along. **A robin watched from its perch,**

head tilted as if to say, 'Come along, now.' She dipped beneath arching branches and climbed over moss-covered stones until she reached a place she'd never seen before: **A clearing, soft with golden light.**

It was as though the forest had **exhaled a secret, and only Willa was meant to hear it.** In the center of the clearing stood a single oak tree, its leaves still clinging stubbornly to their branches while all the others had shed theirs. Beneath it, nestled in the roots like a forgotten treasure, lay **a weathered wooden sign: The Garden of Forgotten Names.**

Willa's heart skipped, and just as she stepped closer, **a flicker of movement caught her eye—a flash of something small, quick, and shimmering, like sunlight glinting off a dewdrop.**

"Oi! Mind where you step, girl!"

A tiny figure zipped into view, hovering just above Willa's head. It was **no bigger than a mouse**, with wings that shimmered like dragonfly glass. **The fairy was dressed in a haphazard tunic made of petals and moss**, and her wild copper hair stuck out in every direction. She planted her hands on her hips and fixed Willa with a mischievous grin.

"You almost squashed me! And I've not been properly squashed in ages!"

Willa blinked in surprise. **"Are you... a fairy?"**

The tiny creature gave a dramatic bow, wings fluttering like a leaf caught in a breeze. **"Larkspur, at your service! Purveyor of pranks, seeker of shiny things, and professional 'not-getting-squashed' enthusiast!"** She paused, tilting her head as if studying Willa closely. "And you must be... hmm... Willa. Yes, yes, I can smell a lost name on you."

"A lost name?" Willa whispered, her heart fluttering like a moth's wings.

Larkspur grinned wider, her eyes glittering like morning dew. **"That's what you're missing, isn't it? Not just the necklace. Oh no, love—it's more than that. You've lost a little piece of yourself, too. And lucky for you, this forest loves finding what's been lost."**

Willa opened her mouth to reply, but **a sudden rustling sound stole the words from her lips.** Something—or someone—was coming. **The underbrush shivered and parted, revealing a sleek fox with fur the color of autumn leaves and eyes as sharp as amber stones.**

"Well, well," the fox said with a polite nod, his voice smooth as warm cider. **"It seems we have a guest. Welcome to the Forest of Forgotten Names, my dear. I am Mr. Tawnycoat, proprietor of the finest burrow inn on this side of the hill."** He bowed low, his tail curling elegantly over his paws.

Willa gave a small curtsy in return, feeling oddly as if she'd stepped into one of her grandmother's old stories. **"I think I've lost something,"** she admitted softly. **"I don't know how to find it."**

Larkspur buzzed beside her ear. **"That's where we come in, darling! This place is full of forgotten things. And if you ask the right questions, the forest might just show you what you need."**

Mr. Tawnycoat gave a thoughtful hum, his whiskers twitching. **"The garden will help, yes, but only if it feels like helping. It's a bit... selective."**

"Selective?" Willa asked.

"**Picky as an old cat,**" Larkspur chimed in with a wink. "**You've got to give it something in return—something true. A promise, maybe. Or a story.**" Willa hesitated, the words tasting strange on her tongue. "**What kind of story?**"

Mr. Tawnycoat's amber eyes twinkled. "**The kind only you can tell. But don't fret—stories have a way of finding themselves, just like lost names.**"

Just then, **the air shifted**, and the clearing grew warmer, as though the very ground beneath her feet was listening. **A leaf drifted lazily from the oak's branches**, golden and perfect, landing softly in Willa's open palm.

And there, written on the leaf in tiny, elegant script, was a name—**not her own, but someone else's.** Willa traced the letters with her fingertip, feeling the hum of magic beneath them. "**Elspeth...**" she whispered, the name unfurling in her heart like a forgotten melody.

"**Ah, the first piece of the puzzle,**" Larkspur said with a grin. "**Good start! Now, let's hope the garden's feeling generous today.**"

Mr. Tawnycoat gave a solemn nod. "**There's no time to waste. The magic here is thinning. If we don't restore it before winter's first frost, this place will fade away... and everything lost within it will be lost for good.**"

Willa tightened her grip on the leaf, determination sparking in her chest. "**Then I guess we'd better find the rest of the names.**" Larkspur clapped her hands. "**Now you're thinking! But first, we'll need Bramble.**"

"**Bramble?**" Willa asked, her brow furrowing.

The fairy gave a sly smile. "**Oh, you'll love her. She's got a way with words... and curses. Lives up in the pine trees, does** a bit of knitting, a bit of spell-casting, and makes the best hazelnut tea this side of the forest."

Mr. Tawnycoat flicked his tail. "And she doesn't suffer fools, so we'd best be on our way before she decides we're more trouble than we're worth."

With that, Larkspur zipped off toward the trees, trailing sparkles like a comet in the dusk. Mr. Tawnycoat gave Willa a knowing look. "Best keep up, dear. This story is just getting started. And that goes for you too, yes YOU! The one reading this, Keep up!"

And with **a rustle of leaves and a ripple of laughter**, Willa followed the fox and the fairy into the heart of the forest, the golden leaf tucked safely in her pocket—**the first of many names waiting to be found.**

And so, the adventure began.

Bramble in the Pines

The forest grew thicker as they ventured deeper, the air laced with the sharp scent of pine needles and the sweet hint of frost waiting just beyond the horizon. **Sunlight filtered through the treetops in long, golden ribbons**, lighting their way as Larkspur darted ahead, her wings shimmering like mist over morning meadows.

Willa's boots crunched through carpets of pinecones and brittle leaves, and Mr. Tawnycoat padded beside her with quiet grace, his amber eyes alert. Somewhere in the distance, **a jay let out a scolding cry**, and the wind whispered through the branches, carrying secrets only trees could understand.

"Mind your step here," Mr. Tawnycoat advised, flicking his tail. **"Bramble's treehouse isn't exactly fond of uninvited guests."** Willa raised an eyebrow. **"It's a treehouse. How bad could it be?"**

Larkspur spun in midair and grinned. **"Bad enough to turn your boots into mushrooms if you don't behave."** She gave a gleeful laugh, her wings twinkling like frost-kissed petals. **"Bramble doesn't take kindly to nonsense, but if she likes you—oh, she might knit you a scarf or two."**

Willa's pulse quickened as they reached the **edge of a dense grove**, the trees pressed close as though guarding something precious. From high above, **a plume of smoke curled through the branches, carrying the smell of hazelnut and clove.**

"There it is." Mr. Tawnycoat nodded toward the towering pine, its trunk wide enough to house a dozen foxes. **A crooked ladder made of twisted roots wound upward**, vanishing into the canopy. "Up we go."

Willa craned her neck, squinting to see where the ladder ended. **"Is it safe?"** Mr. Tawnycoat gave her a look that suggested **safety wasn't really the point. "It won't drop you unless it takes offense. Try not to insult it."**

Before Willa could ask what counted as an insult to a ladder, **Larkspur zipped to the top, calling down, "Come on, slowpokes! The tea's not going to drink itself!"**

Taking a deep breath, Willa placed her foot on the first rung. **The roots shifted beneath her weight, groaning like an old rocking chair**, but they held firm. She climbed carefully, Mr. Tawnycoat following with ease. As they rose higher, the forest spread beneath them like a sea of gold and green, the leaves shimmering in the afternoon light.

When they reached the top, **the treehouse came into view**: a ramshackle cottage woven from branches and bark, tucked snugly into the crook of the pine tree. **Smoke puffed from a stone chimney**, and bundles of herbs—sage, thyme, and lavender—hung from the rafters. **Glass jars filled with glowing fireflies lined the windows**, casting a warm, flickering glow.

"Bramble's place," Larkspur announced with a dramatic wave of her hand. **"Cozy, isn't it?"** Before Willa could respond, **the door creaked open, and a figure stepped out.**

Bramble was not what Willa expected. She was **short and round**, with silver hair piled high in a messy bun, her hands dusted with flour as if she'd just stepped away from baking. **Her eyes, sharp as frost on a windowpane, narrowed as she looked them over.** She wore a patchwork dress and a woolen shawl draped over her shoulders.

"Well now," Bramble muttered, dusting her hands on her apron. **"What's all this, then? A fairy, a fox, and..."** Her gaze landed on Willa, and her lips pursed. **"A human, hmm? Haven't seen one of those in quite a while."**

Larkspur flew forward, perching on Bramble's shoulder with a wide grin. **"Brought you some company, Bramble! Thought you might like a change of pace."**

Bramble gave the fairy a withering look, though her eyes twinkled with the faintest hint of affection. **"Did you, now? Thought you'd bring me trouble more like."** She turned her attention back to Willa, eyeing her up and down as if weighing her on invisible scales. **"Well, you've got leaves in your hair and mud on your boots. Could be worse."**

Willa shuffled nervously, unsure what to say. "I... I lost something." Bramble snorted. **"We all have, dearie. The forest's full of lost things. The trick is knowing which ones are worth finding."** Willa pulled the golden leaf from her pocket and held it out. **"I found this."**

Bramble's eyes widened slightly, and she took the leaf with surprising gentleness. **"Elspeth,"** she whispered, her voice softer now. **"Well, I'll be. I thought that name was gone for good."** She looked at Willa with new interest. **"Maybe you've got more sense in you than I gave you credit for."**

Larkspur clapped her hands. **"See? I told you she was special!"** Bramble huffed, though there was a hint of a smile at the corners of her mouth. **"Come inside, then. We'd best get to work. Winter's not waiting, and neither is this garden."**

The inside of the treehouse was every bit as magical as Willa had imagined. **A cozy fire crackled in the hearth**, casting flickering shadows across walls lined with books, jars, and baskets. **Bundles of herbs dangled from the ceiling**, and the air smelled of warm bread, pine resin, and hazelnut tea.

Bramble busied herself at the stove, pouring tea into mismatched mugs. **"Right, then. If you're going to save this garden, you'll need more than luck. Names are tricky things. They have power, and you can't just pluck them from thin air."**

Willa sipped her tea, the warmth spreading through her like sunlight on a cold morning. **"How do I find the other names?"**

Bramble gave a wry smile. **"Ah, that's the fun part. The names are hidden in the forest—tucked inside dreams, folded into songs, or etched on the backs of leaves. Some are guarded by creatures who won't part with them easily."**

Larkspur buzzed excitedly. **"Oh! We'll get to meet the toadstool singers! And the snoring willow!"** Mr. Tawnycoat chuckled softly. **"Don't forget the blackberry brambles. They're quite the gossip."** Willa's heart lifted at the thought of the adventure ahead. **"And if we find all the names... will the garden's magic come back?"**

Bramble stirred her tea thoughtfully. **"If the forest thinks it's worth it, yes. But it won't be easy, child. Some things—once forgotten—aren't so eager to be remembered."**

Larkspur flitted to Willa's shoulder and gave her a playful nudge. **"Don't worry! We've got tea, stories, and a fox with excellent manners. What could possibly go wrong?"**

Mr. Tawnycoat raised an eyebrow but said nothing, though **his eyes twinkled with amusement.** Bramble set down her mug and dusted off her hands. **"Well, if we're going to do this, we'd best start now. Winter waits for no one."**

Willa nodded, feeling a flicker of hope settle in her chest like a glowing ember. **The garden was fading, but perhaps—just perhaps—it wasn't too late to bring it back to life.**

With a rustle of pine needles and a swirl of magic, the adventure truly began.

The Toadstool Singers and the Gossiping Brambles

The forest thickened as the air changed. A hint of magic flowed through a breeze. It no longer carried the sharpness of pine needles or the warmth of cinnamon—it was richer now, **thick with the scent of damp moss and turned earth**, like an old book long forgotten in an attic. Willa's breath puffed in little clouds as the afternoon dimmed, and even the sound of her steps softened beneath the blanket of fallen leaves. Somewhere ahead, **a lilting melody drifted through the trees**, light as bubbles on a breeze.

"Do you hear that?" Willa whispered. Mr. Tawnycoat's ears perked, and he gave a knowing hum. **"Ah, the toadstool singers. You'll like them—charming little fellows with a fondness for music."**

"And terrible at knowing when to stop," Larkspur added, spinning through the air. She flitted ahead, her wings a blur of motion. **"It's like they're enchanted to keep singing unless someone sneezes or gives them a riddle they can't answer. Personally, I prefer the sneezing. Much faster."**

Willa tucked her hands into the pockets of her jacket as the path grew narrower, branches pressing close like curious onlookers. The wind stirred around her, lifting stray leaves into lazy spirals.

Suddenly, the forest opened into a small **clearing bathed in soft green light.** In the center, nestled beneath a ring of ferns, sat **a perfect circle of red-capped toadstools**, their spots as white as freshly fallen snow. And perched on top of each toadstool was a tiny creature, **each no taller than Willa's thumb**, with wrinkled faces and hats shaped like the little mushrooms they sat upon.

They sang in perfect harmony:

"A traveler bold and a traveler small,
Find the song that hides us all!
La-la, la-la, a tale in the breeze,
A name to carry on autumn's leaves!"

Willa stopped at the edge of the clearing, mesmerized by the way the song **twirled and danced** through the air, wrapping around her like a cozy blanket. **The singers swayed side to side,** their tiny feet tapping the edges of their toadstools in rhythm.

"Aren't they just delightful?" Larkspur whispered. Willa smiled. **"I didn't know mushrooms could sing."**

"Technically," Mr. Tawnycoat murmured with a twitch of his whiskers, **"they're sprites who prefer mushrooms. Quite particular about their seats, in fact. Ask them to sit anywhere else, and you'll never hear the end of it."**

Just then, **the singing stopped.** The little sprites turned as one to face Willa, their bright eyes twinkling with curiosity.

"New ears! New ears!" they cried, bouncing excitedly on their toadstools. **"Come close, come near, a song for your cheer!"**

Willa stepped carefully into the circle, enchanted by the tiny creatures. As she did, the toadstool singers began again, their voices weaving a melody that sounded both familiar and strange, like a lullaby half-remembered from childhood.

"In forests deep where lost names grow,
We sing to those who wish to know.
A leaf that falls, a wind that flies,
A name that hides behind the skies..."

Their song trailed off, and the sprite on the tallest toadstool leaned forward, **squinting at Willa with beady eyes. "What name do you seek, little wanderer?"**

Willa hesitated, the question hanging in the air. **What name did she seek?** It wasn't just the acorn necklace she had lost—**it was something deeper, something hidden beneath layers of memory and time.** "I don't know yet," she admitted softly, **the words tasting like autumn rain on her tongue.**

The sprites murmured amongst themselves, their tiny voices buzzing like bees. **"A name unknown! A story untold!"**

"Perhaps she needs a hint!" suggested one sprite. **"Perhaps a clue!"** cried another.

But before they could launch into another song, **a sharp rustling sound came from the thicket at the edge of the clearing.** The toadstool singers froze, their tiny mouths clamping shut. Even Larkspur stopped fluttering, hovering mid-air with a suspicious frown.

"Oh no," Mr. Tawnycoat muttered, his tail flicking in irritation. "Not them." The ferns shivered, and from the underbrush slithered **a tangled mass of blackberry brambles,** their thorny vines twisting and curling like mischievous snakes.

The brambles swayed toward the circle, their dark berries glistening ominously in the dim light.

"We heard a song, we did!" one of the brambles whispered, its voice a dry hiss. "Words upon the wind... juicy words, delicious words..."

Willa took a step back as the brambles encroached upon the clearing, their thorny tips reaching hungrily toward the sprites. The toadstool singers shrank back, their tiny hats trembling with fear.

"We only share stories, not gossip!" one sprite protested. "Stories, gossip—what's the difference?" the brambles hissed, weaving closer. "Tell us what the wind said. What did the Zephyr bring today?"

Willa's heart quickened. The Zephyr—the wind that steals words. She remembered Mr. Tawnycoat's warning about it earlier. "Do you know where it is?" Willa asked urgently. "The Zephyr?"

The brambles tittered, their thorny vines shivering with dark amusement. "Oh, it's nearby... it always is. Listening, waiting, hungry for words..."

Before Willa could ask more, a sudden gust of wind whipped through the clearing, scattering leaves and snatching up the last notes of the toadstool song. "There it is!" Larkspur cried, zipping through the air. "The Zephyr!"

The wind spiraled around them in a mischievous whirl, plucking at Willa's hair and lifting Larkspur higher into the air. Words sparkled on the breeze—stolen fragments of conversations, snatches of forgotten lullabies, pieces of lost names—all tangled together like a glittering net.

"Give those back!" Willa shouted, but her words were snatched mid-sentence, spiraling into the wind and vanishing. Mr. Tawnycoat gave an exasperated sigh. "You see? I told you—sticky fingers, that wind."

The toadstool singers tried to start another song, but the Zephyr spun through the clearing again, stealing their words before they could finish a single verse.

"We'll never get anywhere like this," Bramble muttered. "We'll have to trap it."

"How do you trap a wind?" Willa asked, her voice half-stolen by the swirling breeze. Bramble smirked. "With a riddle." Bramble gathered the group in a huddle, her eyes sparkling with mischief. "Wind can't resist a good riddle," she explained. "It'll get so caught up trying to solve it that it won't notice it's being tied down."

"And who's good at riddles?" Larkspur asked, arching an eyebrow. Bramble grinned. "I am." The Zephyr swirled closer, drawn by the murmured conversation, its invisible hands plucking at loose threads of sound.

"Ready?" Bramble whispered to the group.

Willa nodded, gripping the golden leaf in her pocket. Bramble stood tall and addressed the wind, her voice clear and steady. "Tell me, Zephyr, what flies without wings, sings without a voice, and dances without feet?"

The wind hesitated, faltering mid-swirl. It spun in place, as if puzzled, the stolen words hovering uncertainly in the air. "Aha!" Larkspur whispered gleefully. "It's hooked!"

The Zephyr twisted and turned, struggling to unravel the riddle. While it was distracted, the toadstool singers began humming a quiet melody, weaving their song into the breeze, tangling the wind in a net of notes.

Willa could feel the shift—the way the forest seemed to lean in, holding its breath. The Zephyr slowed, caught between the music and the riddle, its grip on the stolen words loosening.

"A shadow," Bramble whispered softly. "The answer is a shadow." And with that, **the wind sighed, defeated.** It released its stolen treasures—words, stories, and names—letting them drift gently to the ground like autumn leaves.

As the wind stilled, **a single word floated toward Willa,** shimmering in the fading light. She reached out, catching it gently in her palm.

The word was "Elspeth."

Willa traced the letters with her finger, feeling a strange warmth bloom in her chest. **"Elspeth..." she whispered.** It wasn't her name, but it felt familiar, like the echo of a story she had once known.

Mr. Tawnycoat gave a satisfied nod. **"One name down. Many more to go."** Larkspur clapped her hands, sending a shower of sparkles into the air. **"And that's how you outsmart a wind!"**

Willa tucked the name safely into her pocket, her heart lighter than it had been in days. **The forest felt different now—more alive, more hopeful.**

But there was still much to do, and winter's frost was drawing closer. **"Come on,"** Bramble said, **adjusting her shawl. "We've got more names to find, and the forest won't wait."**

With the riddle solved and the Zephyr defeated—for now—the group pressed on, their spirits high and their hearts filled with the promise of stories waiting to be found.

A Wind That Steals Words

The sky above the forest deepened into hues of dusky gold and soft lavender as Willa and her companions continued along the narrow path, **their feet brushing through blankets of fallen leaves that whispered secrets beneath their steps.** The name *Elspeth* lay folded safely in Willa's pocket, its presence a quiet reminder of how much more there was to find—and how little time they had to find it. **The first frost hung on the air like a warning, and the magic of the forest felt thin, stretched at the seams.**

"The Zephyr is a trickster," Mr. Tawnycoat muttered, his ears flicking nervously as they walked. **"It may be quiet now, but don't think it's gone. The wind always comes back."**

Willa tugged her jacket tighter, casting a glance at the shifting trees. **The forest had grown restless,** leaves rustling where no breeze stirred, branches creaking like uneasy whispers. **Larkspur hovered close to Willa's shoulder,** her wings humming softly. Even the fairy, usually so lighthearted, seemed unusually still, her gaze scanning the treetops.

"This part of the forest feels strange," Willa said, rubbing her arms against the chill. **"Like it's holding its breath."**

"That's because it is," Bramble replied, her tone brisk. **"The forest knows what's coming."** She reached into her pocket, pulling out a small satchel of dried herbs, and scattered a pinch of **mugwort and sage along the path.**

"For protection," she explained when she caught Willa's questioning look. **"Zephyrs love to steal what's precious—words, promises, even memories if they're sharp enough."**

Willa felt a knot tighten in her chest. **What if the wind had already taken something from her?** Something she hadn't noticed yet, something essential?

"Stay close," Mr. Tawnycoat advised. **"And keep your words few. The less you say, the less the wind can take."**

They followed the twisting path deeper into the forest, where the trees arched overhead, **their bare branches like the bones of forgotten stories.** The deeper they went, the more the wind began to stir—first as a whisper, then as a sigh, and finally as a playful gust that **curled around their feet and tugged at the edges of Willa's scarf.**

Larkspur shot forward, wings shimmering. "It's back!" she hissed, circling frantically. **"The Zephyr's here!"**

Before anyone could react, **the wind swirled faster, twisting between the branches like a mischievous spirit.** It darted toward Bramble, flicking at the hem of her shawl. It nipped at Mr. Tawnycoat's tail, sending him spinning with a growl. And then it turned toward Willa—**a sudden, invisible force tugging at the edges of her thoughts.**

Words danced on the wind, half-spoken memories and fragments of forgotten sentences:

"The last story... No, not there... It was just a dream..."

Willa gasped, clutching the pocket where the name *Elspeth* was hidden, as if it might slip away. **The Zephyr swirled faster**

now, sensing her fear. It spiraled upward, carrying with it every loose word, every unfinished thought, scattering them into the trees like dry leaves.

"**Not today, you don't!**" Bramble barked. With a swift motion, she tossed a handful of herbs into the wind. **The leaves and petals scattered through the air, glowing faintly as they drifted.**

The Zephyr hesitated, caught between the swirling herbs and the song still lingering in the forest. **For the briefest moment, the air stilled.**

"**Now!**" Mr. Tawnycoat urged. "Speak a word it can't carry! Speak something it can't steal!"

Willa thought fast, her heart hammering in her chest. **What word couldn't the Zephyr steal?** Every word she knew seemed fragile in the face of the wind, easily plucked away like petals from a flower.

And then she remembered. Not a word—but a name. A name the forest had given her. A name that carried weight, like an anchor in a storm.

She cupped her hands around her mouth and whispered: "**Elspeth.**"

The sound of the name seemed to **hum through the clearing**, resonating with the trees and the earth beneath her feet. The Zephyr swirled violently, trying to grasp the name, but **it slipped through its grasp like water.** The name had roots—it belonged to the forest now, not the wind.

The Zephyr hissed in frustration, spiraling higher into the sky until **it vanished, leaving the clearing silent and still.**

Willa exhaled sharply and **The forest seemed to exhale with her,** the tension easing from the branches and the leaves settling into a gentle rustle. Mr. Tawnycoat shook out his fur with a satisfied huff.

"**Well done, child,**" Bramble said, giving Willa an approving nod. "**That was quick thinking.**"

"**I'll admit,**" Larkspur added with a grin, "**you're braver than I gave you credit for.**" She twirled in the air, her wings catching the light. "**Most people panic when a wind tries to steal their words.**"

Willa smiled, though her heart was still racing. **She felt lighter somehow**, as if naming the stolen word had lifted a weight from her chest. The name *Elspeth* seemed to hum in her pocket, a quiet reminder of the story she was unraveling piece by piece.

"**That's one name safe,**" Mr. Tawnycoat said, glancing toward the path ahead. "**But we've got more to find, and the Zephyr won't be far off for long.**"

"**Onward, then,**" Bramble said, dusting off her hands. "**Before the next breeze comes sniffing around.**"

As they walked, **the forest seemed to shift around them**, welcoming them back into its embrace. **The trees swayed gently,** as if whispering their approval. Somewhere high above, a squirrel chattered cheerfully, and the distant sound of the toadstool singers' song echoed faintly through the branches.

Willa felt a strange sense of belonging as she walked beneath the canopy. **The forest was changing her—little by little, leaf by leaf.** She had entered the woods searching for something lost, but **she was finding pieces of herself instead, scattered like breadcrumbs along the path.**

And then she saw it.

A cluster of leaves hanging low on a branch, their edges curled and golden. **Words were etched into the veins**, faint but unmistakable:

"Find the acorn, and you'll find the heart."

Willa stopped in her tracks, staring at the message. **"The acorn..."** she whispered. It was talking about her necklace—the one her grandmother had given her. The one she had lost.

Bramble noticed the change in Willa's expression and followed her gaze. **"Ah,"** she murmured. **"The forest always leaves clues, if you know where to look."**

Willa's heart quickened. **"Do you think the acorn is part of the magic? Part of what's making the forest fade?"**

"Could be," Mr. Tawnycoat said thoughtfully. **"Or it could be something even more important."**

The message on the leaves filled Willa with a new sense of determination. **The acorn wasn't just a necklace—it was part of her story, part of the forest's story.** And if she could find it, maybe she could unravel the rest of the mystery.

"We have to keep going," Willa said, her voice steady with resolve. **"We have to find the rest of the names—and the acorn. Before it's too late."**

Larkspur gave a cheerful clap. **"That's the spirit! Adventure waits for no one, after all."**

Bramble adjusted her shawl with a satisfied nod. **"Onward, then. There's still plenty of forest left, and winter's not waiting."**

And so they pressed on, **the forest welcoming them deeper into its heart.** The path stretched ahead, winding through shadows and light, leading them toward the next chapter of their adventure—and the next name waiting to be found.

The wind stirred gently behind them, but this time, it felt more like a friend than a foe—**as if the forest itself was rooting for them, quietly cheering them on.**

And Willa knew, in her heart, that the forest wasn't done with her yet. **Not by a long shot.**

The Snoring Willow and the Night of Dreams

The shadows lengthened as Willa, Bramble, Mr. Tawnycoat, and Larkspur pressed deeper into the forest. **The trees grew taller, their branches arching like ribs of a great beast, forming a tunnel of twilight.** Ahead, a soft light glimmered through the mist, and the air took on a heavy, dreamy quality—**as if the forest itself was on the verge of sleep.**

"**We're close,**" Bramble whispered, her sharp eyes scanning the path ahead. "**The Snoring Willow isn't far. We'll rest there, and if the tree likes us, it might lend us one of its dreams.**"

"**Do trees dream?**" Willa asked, keeping her voice low. "**Oh, absolutely,**" Larkspur said, spinning in lazy circles. "**But their dreams are strange. They're not like ours—they're slower, heavier. You have to pay close attention, or you'll get lost in them.**"

"**And that's if the tree's in a good mood,**" Mr. Tawnycoat added with a flick of his tail. "**If not, well... let's just say it's best to avoid waking it up on the wrong side of its roots.**"

The group fell into a quiet rhythm, **the forest's silence pressing gently around them like a blanket of fog.** Willa felt a strange sense of calm settle over her, despite the weight of the task ahead. **The Zephyr's threat still lingered in the back of her**

mind, but for now, the forest seemed at peace, and she let herself breathe in the cool, pine-scented air.

At last, the path opened into a small **clearing bathed in silver moonlight**, where an ancient willow tree stood, its drooping branches swaying like a curtain of whispers. **The bark glowed faintly with a greenish hue, as though moss had grown along its surface, and the soft, rhythmic sound of snoring rumbled from deep within its roots.**

Willa stared in awe. **"It's beautiful."**

"And temperamental," Bramble warned, pulling a jar of moonwater from her pocket. **"The trick is to ask nicely."**

Larkspur zipped toward the tree, landing lightly on one of the hanging branches. **"Good evening, old friend!"** she called, her voice cheerful but respectful. **"Mind if we stay a while?"**

The tree gave a long, groaning sigh, its branches swaying in response. **A deep, rumbling voice drifted up from the roots, as slow and heavy as the shifting of mountains.**

"Mmm… travelers. What do you seek?"

"We're looking for dreams," Willa said, taking a step forward. **"A dream that might hold a name we've lost."**

The willow shifted, and the ground beneath Willa's feet seemed to hum with quiet energy. **The tree's branches curled inward, cradling the group in a soft cocoon of leaves.**

"Sleep," the willow murmured. **"And if the forest wills it… a dream will come."**

Willa settled down at the base of the tree, resting her head against the smooth, moss-covered trunk. **The night air was cool but not cold, and the willow's soft snores created a lullaby that drifted through the clearing.** Mr. Tawnycoat curled up beside her, his fur warm against her leg, and Larkspur buzzed softly, settling into a nook between two branches.

Bramble adjusted her shawl and leaned back, closing her eyes. **"Sleep well,"** she whispered. **"Dream wisely."**

And then, slowly, Willa drifted off to sleep, carried on the soft rustling of leaves and the faint hum of moonlight.

Willa found herself standing in **a house with no doors and no windows**, the walls made of twisting branches and roots. The only light came from a **silver acorn resting on a wooden table**, glowing softly in the darkness. She reached for it, but as soon as her fingers brushed the surface, **the acorn split open**, revealing a tiny, glowing name inside:

"Rowan."

Before she could pick it up, the acorn shattered into silver dust, and the dream shifted. **The walls melted away**, replaced by a forest that seemed both familiar and strange. **She heard laughter—her own laughter, from years ago—and the sound of her grandmother's voice, distant but comforting.**

"You'll always find your way, my little Willa," the voice whispered. **"Even when you think you're lost, the forest will remember you."**

Willa turned toward the sound, but the dream slipped away like water through her fingers, and the forest faded into darkness.

Willa awoke to **the soft light of dawn filtering through the willow's branches.** The air smelled of damp earth and wildflowers, and the snoring had quieted to a gentle hum.

As she sat up, **something small and light drifted down from the tree's branches, landing softly in her lap.** It was a leaf—golden and perfect—with a single word written along its veins:

"Rowan."

Willa traced the letters with her fingertip, feeling a strange warmth spread through her chest. **It wasn't her name, but it felt like a piece of a story she was slowly piecing together.**

"Another name found," Mr. Tawnycoat murmured, blinking sleepily. **"Well done."**

Larkspur stretched her wings with a yawn. **"That's two names—Elspeth and Rowan. Not bad for a night's work!"**

"The forest is on our side," Bramble said, brushing leaves from her shawl. **"But we're far from done."**

Willa tucked the golden leaf into her pocket, her heart lighter than it had been the day before. **The forest's magic was still thin, but with each name they found, it felt a little stronger—a little more whole.**

As they prepared to leave the willow's clearing, Willa felt a flicker of hope stir in her chest. **The Zephyr might still be out there, waiting to steal what it could, but now she had something it couldn't take: the names she carried, the stories she was beginning to remember.**

"We'll find the acorn," she whispered to herself, the promise settling like a spark inside her. **"And we'll bring the magic back."**

The forest rustled around her, as if it had heard her promise and approved. **The journey was far from over, but Willa knew now that she wasn't truly lost.** Not as long as the forest remembered her.

And not as long as she kept believing in its magic.

Lanterns in the Fog

As the group left the clearing behind, **the forest deepened, the trees pressing close, their branches twisting like skeletal hands locked in whispers.** The sunlight, soft and dappled moments ago, vanished behind a sudden veil of mist that rolled through the woods, thick as a dream.

"Careful now," Bramble warned, pulling her shawl tighter. "Fog like this doesn't just wander in without reason."

"It's not the good kind of fog either," Mr. Tawnycoat muttered, his amber eyes narrowing. "This one's carrying a secret with it."

The mist thickened until **the path vanished entirely beneath swirls of white and gray,** leaving the forest suspended in a hazy silence. **Every sound—every rustle of leaves, every snap of a twig—was swallowed by the fog,** as if the mist had a hunger for noise. Willa stayed close to Mr. Tawnycoat, her fingers brushing the soft fur along his back for comfort.

Larkspur darted ahead, her wings flickering like tiny lanterns. "Well, if we're going to get lost in fog, we might as well do it in style."

Willa squinted into the mist. **"How do we know which way to go?"**

Before anyone could answer, a soft, eerie glow appeared ahead—a **flickering, golden light drifting like a**

will-o'-the-wisp through the haze. It bobbed gently, as if inviting them to follow. Then another light appeared, and another, until **a trail of glowing orbs dotted the misty path.**

"Foxfire," Mr. Tawnycoat said softly, his tail flicking in recognition.

Willa took a cautious step forward. **"What's foxfire?"**

"Lanterns made by glowing creatures," he explained. **"Mostly spirits, sometimes enchanted animals. It's best not to ignore them when they show up. They always have a reason."**

Bramble gave a grunt of approval. **"And if we're lucky, they might lead us to something useful. Stay close, though—sometimes foxfire lights the way, and sometimes it leads you straight into trouble."**

The group followed the foxfire trail deeper into the fog, the glowing lights growing brighter the farther they walked. **The mist swirled like river currents,** and soon the dim outlines of creatures began to take shape—**small animals with glowing eyes, carrying tiny acorn lanterns between their teeth or clutched in tiny paws.**

Willa gasped as a **glowing hare bounded past,** trailing sparkles of light with each leap. **A pair of owls floated overhead,** their feathers shining like embers in the mist. Squirrels scampered along the tree branches, carrying tiny lanterns made of hollowed-out acorns with flickering beetles inside.

"It's a foxfire festival," Larkspur whispered, her voice brimming with excitement. **"They do this sometimes when the forest feels... unsettled."**

Willa smiled, enchanted by the sight. **The glowing creatures moved gracefully through the fog, their soft lantern light** casting dancing shadows along the forest floor. It was beautiful—and a little strange, like a dream she wasn't entirely sure she wanted to wake from.

"Look," Mr. Tawnycoat said, his voice low with reverence. He pointed his nose toward the heart of the festival, where a small clearing had opened up beneath the trees.

In the center of the clearing stood a great stone pillar, covered in moss and tangled ivy. At the base of the pillar rested a series of carved runes, glowing faintly in the lantern light. And on top of the stone, glinting like moonlight on water, sat a small, silver acorn—whole and gleaming.

Willa's heart leaped in her chest. "The acorn!" she whispered, stepping forward. "It's here!"

But as soon as she reached the edge of the clearing, Bramble caught her by the shoulder, pulling her back.

"Not so fast, girl," the witch warned, her eyes sharp. "That acorn isn't what it seems."

Willa hesitated, her gaze flickering between the silver acorn and Bramble's stern expression. "What do you mean? It's the same one from my dream, isn't it?"

Bramble nodded slowly. "It is. But things in dreams aren't always whole when you find them awake."

Mr. Tawnycoat sniffed the air cautiously. "I smell a trick."

Before Willa could ask what kind of trick, the silver acorn began to pulse with light, flickering in time with the foxfire lanterns. The mist around the clearing thickened, and the runes at the base of the stone began to glow brighter, casting strange, twisting shadows across the forest floor.

"It's enchanted," Larkspur whispered, her wings fluttering nervously. "Something's protecting it—something old."

Just as the group stepped back from the acorn, **a shadow moved through the fog—sleek and graceful.** From the mist emerged a **large, glowing fox**, its fur shimmering like starlight. In its mouth, it carried a tiny lantern shaped from a hollowed acorn, the light inside flickering softly.

"A guardian," Mr. Tawnycoat whispered in awe, bowing his head in respect. **"I didn't think they still existed."**

The glowing fox set the lantern gently at the base of the stone and sat back on its haunches, regarding Willa with ancient, knowing eyes. **Its gaze was both kind and fierce**, as though it had seen centuries pass and carried all their stories in its heart.

"If you seek the acorn, you must give something in return," the fox said, its voice deep and resonant, like the sound of wind through hollow trees. **"A story for a story. A name for a name."**

Willa stepped forward, her heart pounding. **"I... I don't know what to give,"** she admitted, her voice barely above a whisper.

The fox tilted its head. **"You already carry it with you."**

Willa reached into her pocket, her fingers brushing the golden leaves with the names etched into them: *Elspeth, Rowan.* She knew what she had to do.

"I offer you the name Rowan," she whispered, holding the leaf out toward the fox. **"It isn't mine, but it's part of the story I'm trying to find."**

The fox gave a solemn nod and accepted the leaf between its teeth. **The runes at the base of the stone shifted, glowing brighter for a moment—then fading into soft, pulsing light.**

With the runes dimmed, Willa reached for the silver acorn. **Her fingers trembled as she picked it up**, and the moment it touched her skin, a strange warmth spread through her.

A voice echoed in her mind, faint and familiar:

"The acorn carries what you lost, but it will not mend itself. Only when all the names are found can the forest bloom again."

Willa clutched the acorn tightly, her heart filled with both hope and uncertainty. **The acorn was only part of the answer—there were still more names to find, more pieces of the story waiting to be uncovered.**

"We're not done yet," Bramble said, her voice quiet but firm. **"But this is a start."**

The glowing fox gave a slow, graceful bow and melted back into the mist, its lantern flickering one last time before it vanished. The fog began to lift, and the forest stirred awake, as though shaking off the last remnants of a dream.

Willa tucked the silver acorn safely into her pocket, alongside the golden leaves with their etched names. **The forest seemed brighter now, the air lighter.** The path ahead was still long, but for the first time, Willa felt certain they were moving in the right direction.

"Come on," Larkspur said with a grin, zipping through the thinning mist. **"There's more magic out there waiting to be found!"**

Mr. Tawnycoat gave a satisfied flick of his tail. **"And more stories to tell."**

Bramble adjusted her shawl and gave Willa an approving nod. **"Onward, then. The forest hasn't given up on us yet."**

And so they continued down the winding path, **the lanterns of foxfire glowing gently behind them**, guiding them toward the next part of their journey—and the next name waiting to be found.

The Tree of Lost Things

The mist had long lifted by the time Willa and her companions approached **the Tree of Lost Things.** The forest around them opened into a wide glade bathed in twilight, where the trees seemed to hold their breath, their branches swaying slowly as if in anticipation. And there, at the very center of the clearing, stood **a towering oak, ancient and immense**, its branches heavy with forgotten treasures.

"This is it," Bramble whispered. **"The Tree of Lost Things. Every item left behind, every memory misplaced, and every promise broken finds its way here."**

Willa stared, her heart racing. **Dangling from the branches like ornaments were thousands of lost objects:** tarnished pocket watches, ribbons, small dolls, toys with missing eyes, weathered notebooks, and pieces of jewelry—each one a fragment of someone's story. And there, nestled among the tangled branches high above, hung **her acorn necklace**, the one her grandmother had given her.

"There it is," Willa whispered, pointing. "My acorn." Larkspur buzzed beside her ear. **"You really did lose something important."**

Mr. Tawnycoat flicked his tail thoughtfully. "The Tree doesn't just keep things for safekeeping," he warned. **"There's always a price for taking something back."**

Bramble gave a grim nod. **"You'll have to trade a memory for the necklace. And not just any memory—a cherished one."**

Willa swallowed hard. **"What kind of memory?"** Bramble's gaze softened slightly. **"The Tree will know. It always knows."**

Willa took a deep breath and stepped closer to the great oak. **Its bark felt warm under her palm, as though the tree were alive in ways beyond nature.** A low hum thrummed beneath her fingertips, and the branches seemed to shift, drawing the acorn necklace closer but keeping it just out of reach.

"What will you offer?" the Tree whispered, its voice deep and resonant, like the creak of wood under heavy snow. **"What memory will you trade?"**

Willa closed her eyes, **her heart tightening painfully.** Memories fluttered through her mind—her grandmother's voice, the sound of her laughter, the feel of her warm hands brushing hair from Willa's face. **There were so many moments she wanted to hold on to, but the Tree demanded one in return for what it kept.**

And then she knew.

The last story her grandmother had ever told her. The one beneath the oak tree on a chilly autumn afternoon, where they'd sat together drinking tea and watching the leaves fall. It was the moment Willa had felt safest, most connected, and she knew it was the memory the Tree wanted. **A memory filled with warmth and love—exactly the kind that the Tree hungered for.**

"I offer the last story my grandmother told me," Willa whispered, **tears stinging her eyes.** The Tree gave a slow groan of approval. **"A worthy trade,"** it murmured.

And just like that, **the memory began to slip away—soft and subtle, like the fading scent of apples left too long on a windowsill.** Willa could still remember her grandmother's face, but the words of the story were already slipping through her fingers, lost to the branches of the Tree.

In return, **the acorn necklace drifted down gently, as if carried on an unseen breeze.** Willa caught it in her hands, the cool weight of the acorn settling into her palm.

She knew the necklace meant something more than she understood yet—something bigger than her. But for now, she tucked it safely into her pocket beside the names she carried: *Elspeth, Rowan.*

As Willa stepped away from the Tree, **the shadows beneath its roots seemed to shift.** For a moment, it looked as though something—or someone—was watching from the tangled mass of roots and stones.

A low, echoing voice drifted up from the ground. "You're not done yet, child. The forest remembers you... but it hasn't forgiven you." Willa froze, her heart pounding. **"What does that mean?"**

Bramble's expression darkened. "The forest holds grudges," she muttered. **"Some promises—once broken—linger longer than others."**

"Come on," Mr. Tawnycoat urged gently, nudging Willa with his nose. **"We've got what we came for. Time to move before the shadows start asking for more."** Larkspur flitted nervously above them, casting glances at the shifting roots. **"I don't like this place," she muttered. **"Too many old stories tangled together."**

Willa hesitated for just a moment longer, but then she followed her friends back to the path, **her fingers tight around the necklace in her pocket.** As they left the clearing behind, **the whispers from the Tree faded into silence,** though their weight still hung heavily in the air.

They walked in silence for a while, the forest around them eerily quiet. **The joy from the foxfire festival felt distant now,** replaced by a somber weight that seemed to settle on Willa's shoulders.

"You did well," Bramble said softly, breaking the silence. **"The Tree doesn't part with things easily. And giving up a memory like that…"** She trailed off, her sharp gaze softening. **"It was a brave thing to do."**

Willa nodded, though her heart ached. **The memory she had traded felt like a part of her—a piece of herself she could never get back.** But she knew it had been the right thing to do. **The acorn necklace wasn't just a keepsake—it was a key to something larger, something she couldn't quite grasp yet. "What now?"** she asked quietly.

"We keep going," Mr. Tawnycoat said. **"There are still more names to find, and the forest isn't done with us yet."**

The path ahead was long, winding through **shifting shadows and glimmers of light,** but Willa felt a flicker of determination rise within her. **The forest had taken something from her—but it had also given something in return.**

She glanced down at the silver acorn nestled in her hand, feeling the smooth curve of its surface beneath her fingertips.

Whatever magic the acorn held, it was hers now—and she would protect it, no matter what.

"We'll find the rest of the names," she whispered, more to herself than anyone else. **"And we'll bring the magic back."**

The wind stirred around her, gentle this time, as though the forest had heard her promise. **The path stretched ahead, waiting for her—and Willa knew she was ready to follow it, wherever it led.**

With her friends beside her and the weight of the past behind her, **Willa took a step forward into the heart of the forest.** The journey wasn't over, but for the first time, she felt certain that she was moving toward something—**something that mattered.**

And the forest, with all its secrets and shadows, whispered quietly in return: **"We are not done with you yet."**

Shadows Beneath the Roots

The forest grew darker as Willa and her companions ventured farther from the Tree of Lost Things. **The path, once open and dappled with soft light, narrowed into a tunnel of branches that seemed to tangle and twist with each step.** It felt as if the forest itself were shifting, growing restless. **The acorn necklace in Willa's pocket hummed faintly,** as though it recognized the place they were headed.

"Something's not right," Mr. Tawnycoat muttered, his **amber eyes flicking toward every rustle in the underbrush.** His fur bristled, and his ears twitched nervously. **"The shadows here... they're thicker than they should be."**

"That's because we're close," Bramble murmured. She traced a finger along the bark of a gnarled tree, where **black tendrils curled through the wood like veins. "The roots of this forest run deep, and not everything down there likes to stay forgotten."**

Willa shivered, clutching the acorn tighter in her hand. **She could feel the weight of the shadows pressing in, old and heavy, like the remnants of a dream she couldn't quite wake from. "Do we have to go underground?"** Willa whispered, glancing nervously at Bramble.

"Afraid so, girl," Bramble said with a grim smile. "If you want to bring back the magic, you've got to confront what's been buried."

They came upon the entrance unexpectedly: **a hollow beneath the roots of a massive oak, the opening barely large enough to crawl through.** The roots tangled above it like a mouth frozen mid-whisper, the earth around it dark and cool.

"**Down we go,**" Bramble said, kneeling to peer inside. "**Stay close. The shadows don't like guests, and if you wander off, they'll keep you.**"

Willa's heart thudded painfully in her chest, but she nodded, steeling herself. **This was part of the journey—something she had to face, no matter how frightening.**

"**I'll go first,**" Mr. Tawnycoat offered. With a quick flick of his tail, he slipped into the hollow, his fur vanishing into the dark like a flicker of smoke.

Larkspur buzzed beside Willa, her wings glowing faintly. "**Come on, kiddo. No shadow's going to keep us down here.**"

Taking a deep breath, **Willa followed them into the hollow,** the cool earth pressing close around her. **The scent of moss and damp stone filled the air,** and as the roots tangled above her, it felt like stepping into another world—a world where light struggled to survive.

They emerged into a vast **underground cavern,** its walls lined with twisting roots and glimmering stones. **The air felt thick and still,** like the moment just before a storm. **In the far corners of the cavern, shadows pooled together,** writhing and shifting as if they had minds of their own. "**This place is... strange,**" Willa whispered, her voice barely carrying through the heavy air.

"That's one way to put it," Bramble muttered. "This is where the forest's broken promises gather. Every fear, every doubt—it all finds its way down here eventually." She gave Willa a sidelong glance. "And it looks like some of yours made the trip, too."

Willa's pulse quickened. "What do you mean?"

Before Bramble could answer, the shadows in the cavern began to stir, drawing together into strange shapes—twisted versions of things Willa recognized.

One shadow flickered into the shape of her grandmother's hand, but when Willa reached out, it crumbled into ash. Another formed into a version of Willa herself, small and frightened, clutching her knees as if hiding from the world.

"That's…" Willa whispered, trailing off.

"That's the part of you that thinks you're not enough," Bramble said softly. "The part that's afraid to lose everything, even the magic."

The shadow-Willa lifted her head, her dark, hollow eyes filled with all the doubts Willa had ever carried.

"You'll never find what you're looking for," the shadow whispered, its voice cold and sharp, like wind against glass. "It's already too late."

Willa stepped back, her breath catching. The cavern seemed to press tighter around her, the shadows growing thicker, darker, whispering doubts into her mind.

"It's just a shadow," Larkspur whispered, landing lightly on Willa's shoulder. "It's not real. It only has the power you give it."

"That's easy for you to say," Willa muttered, swallowing hard. "What if the shadow's right? What if it's too late to save the forest?"

"It's never too late, kiddo," Larkspur said gently. "That's the trick. Shadows lie. You just have to stop believing them."

Willa closed her eyes, the weight of the shadows pressing down on her like cold water. **She could feel the fear curling inside her**, whispering that she wasn't brave enough, that she would never find the magic again. But then she remembered something—**her grandmother's voice, soft and steady, saying:** **"Even when you think you're lost, the forest will remember you."**

Willa took a deep breath and opened her eyes. **The shadows twisted and snarled around her**, but she met their gaze without flinching.

"You're not real," she whispered to the shadow version of herself. **"You don't get to tell me what I can or can't do."**

The shadow faltered, its form flickering like a candle in the wind. **Willa took a step closer, her heart steady now.**

"I may not know everything," she said, her voice growing stronger, **"but I know this: I have friends. I have stories. And I have hope. That's enough."**

With those words, **the shadow crumbled into mist,** dissolving into the earth. **The cavern seemed to sigh in relief,** the weight of the air lifting as the shadows slithered back into the cracks and corners, defeated.

As the last of the shadows disappeared, **something small and glimmering emerged from the roots of the cavern wall—a smooth, black stone inscribed with a single name: "Elowen."**

Willa knelt down, her heart thudding as she traced the letters with her fingertips. **Another name—a piece of the story, waiting to be found.**

"**That's three now,**" Bramble murmured, her voice warm with approval. "**Elspeth, Rowan, and Elowen. You're doing well, girl.**" Mr. Tawnycoat gave a pleased hum. "**Not bad for one night's work.**"

Willa tucked the stone carefully into her pocket, alongside the leaves and the silver acorn. **Her heart felt lighter than it had in days,** as though confronting her fears had given her back a piece of herself she hadn't realized was missing.

They left the cavern behind, climbing back through the hollow and emerging once more into the moonlit forest. **The night air felt cool and fresh**, and the stars glittered above them like tiny lanterns scattered across the sky.

Willa glanced at her companions, feeling a warmth spread through her chest. **The forest was still dangerous, still full of mysteries and challenges—but she wasn't afraid anymore.** Not really. **Not as long as she had her friends beside her, and not as long as she carried the names and stories that mattered.**

"**Let's keep going,**" Willa said softly, adjusting her scarf. "**We've got more names to find—and I think the forest is waiting for us.**"

"**That's the spirit!**" Larkspur cheered, zipping ahead with a trail of sparkles.

Bramble chuckled softly. "**Onward it is, then.**" And so they walked on, **their footsteps light on the forest floor, the night air humming with quiet magic.**

The forest whispered around them, welcoming them back—and somewhere deep within its heart, more names waited to be found.

The Silver Acorn and
the Broken Story

The forest felt different now. **The air shimmered with a quiet sense of expectancy,** as though the trees were leaning closer, waiting to see what Willa and her companions would do next. **The silver acorn in Willa's pocket thrummed softly,** and each step along the path felt heavier with the weight of the magic still left to uncover. **The forest had given them pieces—names, memories, fragments of stories—but nothing felt complete yet.** There were still parts missing, tangled up in the roots of time.

Willa reached into her pocket and ran her thumb over the smooth curve of the silver acorn. **It felt warm, alive in some strange way, like it was waiting—expecting something of her.**

"What do we do with the acorn?" Willa asked as they walked beneath the tall, swaying pines.

Bramble adjusted her shawl, frowning. "The silver acorn is old magic, deep magic. But it's cracked—broken." She glanced at Willa. **"Until it's whole again, it can't give you what you need."**

"How do we fix it?" Willa asked, her fingers tightening around the acorn.

"We'll need to find the heart of the story it belongs to," Bramble said. **"And that means finding the last of the names.**

Without them, the story can't be mended, and neither can the acorn."

"It's like a puzzle," Larkspur mused, spinning lazily through the air. "Except this puzzle might bite back if we get it wrong."

The path wound onward, carpeted with leaves that whispered underfoot, until the forest opened into a wide clearing bathed in soft moonlight. At the center of the clearing stood another ancient oak tree, smaller than the Tree of Lost Things but just as old, its bark silvered with time.

Bramble stopped, her expression shifting. "This is it," she murmured. "The Heartwood Tree."

"Heartwood?" Willa whispered, stepping closer. The name carried a strange weight, as though it held the answer to a question she didn't know she was asking. The acorn in her pocket warmed, a soft pulse of magic radiating from it.

"This tree holds the stories that connect everything," Mr. Tawnycoat explained quietly. "Every promise, every name, every piece of magic in this forest is rooted here."

Willa reached out, placing her hand against the bark. The tree felt warm beneath her palm, and for a moment, it was as though the world stilled around her. A soft hum rose from the ground, like the first notes of a lullaby, and Willa felt a pull deep in her chest—the sense that this was where she was meant to be.

Bramble stepped beside her, placing a gentle hand on Willa's shoulder. "The acorn belongs to the Heartwood," she said softly. "But it's cracked because something important was lost—a piece of the story it carries."

Willa pulled the silver acorn from her pocket and held it in her hands. A faint crack ran along its surface, and the magic within it flickered, dim and fragile. "**What did it lose?**" she whispered, feeling the ache of the missing piece like it was her own.

Mr. Tawnycoat's amber eyes softened. "**It lost its heart—the part that makes the story whole. And without that, the magic of the forest is fading.**"

Larkspur landed lightly on Willa's shoulder, her wings fluttering. "You already have part of the answer, kiddo. It's in the names you found—Elspeth, Rowan, Elowen. They're not just names. They're stories waiting to be remembered."

Willa knelt beneath the Heartwood Tree, cradling the silver acorn in her hands. **The names she carried whispered softly in her mind**, like leaves stirring in a gentle breeze: *Elspeth, Rowan, Elowen...* Each one felt important, like threads woven through the fabric of the forest's magic.

"**How do I mend it?**" she asked quietly, looking up at Bramble. "**You tell the story,**" Bramble answered simply. "**The names, the pieces—they were never really lost. They were just waiting for someone to remember them.**"

Willa took a deep breath and closed her eyes, letting the rhythm of the forest fill her heart. **The silver acorn pulsed gently in her palm**, and as she began to speak, the words flowed from her like water from a spring.

"**Elspeth was the beginning,**" Willa whispered, her voice soft but steady. "**She was the first story—the one who planted the seeds of magic in this forest long ago.**"

The silver acorn glowed faintly, and **the crack along its surface began to fade. "Rowan was the guardian,**" Willa continued. "**The one who protected the forest when the world began to forget.**"

The acorn glimmered brighter, and **the magic within it grew warmer, more alive. "And Elowen was the keeper of names,"** Willa whispered, feeling the weight of the truth settle in her heart. **"She made sure no story was ever truly lost, even when it seemed forgotten."**

With those words, **the silver acorn sealed itself completely,** the crack disappearing as though it had never been. **A soft pulse of magic radiated from it**, filling the clearing with a warm, golden light.

The Heartwood Tree responded immediately. **Its branches shivered with life**, leaves unfurling along its limbs in bursts of green and gold. **The ground beneath Willa's feet hummed with magic**, and the air felt rich and full, like the scent of the first rain after a long drought.

"You did it," Bramble whispered, a rare smile softening her features. **"The story is whole again."**

Larkspur twirled through the air, leaving trails of sparkles behind her. "I knew you had it in you, kiddo!" Mr. Tawnycoat gave a pleased rumble. **"The forest remembers now. And it's ready to bloom again."**

Willa clutched the mended acorn to her chest, tears prickling at the corners of her eyes. **It wasn't just the forest she had helped—it was herself, too.** In remembering the names and telling the story, she had found something she hadn't known she was missing: **the belief that she was part of something bigger, something that mattered.**

As the light from the Heartwood Tree shimmered around them, Willa knew it was time to make a promise of her own. **She knelt at the base of the tree, placing the silver acorn gently among its roots.**

"I promise to keep believing in magic," she whispered. "Even when it's hard. Even when the world forgets."

The Heartwood Tree shivered in response, its branches swaying in quiet approval. "The forest will always remember you, Willa," Bramble said softly. "As long as you carry its stories, it will never fade."

Willa smiled, her heart light and full. The journey wasn't over yet, but for the first time, she felt certain she was exactly where she was meant to be.

As they left the clearing behind, the forest seemed brighter, more alive—the shadows lighter, the air filled with the soft hum of magic restored. Willa walked with her friends at her side, the mended acorn safely tucked in the heart of the forest.

"What now?" Willa asked, glancing at her companions. "Now?" Larkspur grinned. "Now the real adventure begins."

Mr. Tawnycoat gave a satisfied flick of his tail. "And this time, we carry the stories with us."

Bramble chuckled softly. "Onward, girl. There's still magic waiting to be found—and names left to be remembered."

And with that, they stepped forward into the bright, humming forest, ready to follow the winding path wherever it led next. The forest had remembered its stories—and so had Willa.

The Winter Gate

The wind shifted as the group journeyed deeper into the heart of the forest. **The first hint of winter lingered in the air—sharp and cold, like frost creeping across a windowpane.** The forest seemed quieter now, the colors dimming, as though the trees were bracing themselves for the change that was coming.

Willa pulled her jacket tighter, the silver acorn nestled safely in her pocket. **The magic in the forest had begun to awaken,** but it was fragile still, like the last leaves clinging to the branches before the frost claimed them. **The promise of winter pressed down on her—**a reminder that there was still work to do. **The names they'd found—Elspeth, Rowan, Elowen—had mended part of the story, but not all of it.**

"**We're close,**" Bramble murmured, glancing toward the horizon, where **a thin line of frost glittered along the forest floor. "The Winter Gate lies just ahead."**

"**What is the Winter Gate?**" Willa asked, her breath curling in white clouds as she spoke.

"**It's a door, of sorts,**" Mr. Tawnycoat explained. "**A portal that opens only for those who carry the true names of the forest. It marks the boundary between what was and what will be.**"

"**And it only opens once,**" Bramble added grimly. "**Before the first frost falls.**"

Larkspur flitted beside Willa, her wings glowing faintly in the dimming light. "**No pressure, kiddo, but we need that gate to open, or all the names we've found so far will scatter again.**"

The group continued along the path, **the air growing colder with each step.** The leaves beneath their feet sparkled with frost, and thin tendrils of ice crawled up the trunks of the trees. Willa felt the weight of the forest settle around her, heavy with expectation. **Every step forward felt like a step toward something final—something she couldn't turn back from.**

At last, **the path opened into a narrow glade**, and there, standing in the center, was **the Winter Gate**. It shimmered faintly, its frame woven from silver branches twisted together like vines, **covered in frost and glowing with a pale, cold light.**

The gate had no door, only a **curtain of mist that shifted and swirled**, revealing glimpses of what lay beyond—**a world bathed in snow and starlight, where shadows and stories danced together beneath a winter sky.**

"**This is it,**" Bramble whispered. "**The Winter Gate.**" Willa stepped forward, her heart pounding in her chest. **The gate seemed to hum with quiet power,** and as she approached, the mist parted slightly, revealing a shimmering keyhole in the shape of a leaf.

"**How does it work?**" Willa asked softly, her breath clouding the air. "**The gate responds to true names,**" Mr. Tawnycoat explained. "**You'll need to say the names aloud—the ones you found along the way. Only then will the gate open.**"

Willa nodded, pulling the leaves from her pocket, their golden veins glowing faintly in the twilight. **Elspeth. Rowan. Elowen.** She traced the letters with her fingers, feeling the weight of the stories they carried. **These names weren't just words—they were part of the forest's heart, fragments of magic that had been waiting to be remembered.**

"**You're ready,**" Larkspur whispered, her voice soft and steady. "**Just believe in the story you've found.**"

Willa took a deep breath and stepped closer to the gate. **The mist swirled around her, cold and sharp, and the keyhole glimmered expectantly.**

"**Elspeth,**" Willa whispered, the name slipping from her lips like a song remembered at last.

The gate shivered, the silver branches shifting slightly. **A soft pulse of light rippled through the mist,** as if the forest were listening.

"**Rowan,**" Willa continued, her voice steady now. "**The one who guarded the forest.**" The mist swirled faster, and the gate brightened, responding to the name like an old friend reunited after years apart.

"**Elowen,**" Willa whispered, feeling the truth of the name settle in her heart. "**The keeper of names.**"

With that final word, **the gate glowed bright as moonlight,** and the mist parted completely, revealing what lay beyond—a vast, snow-covered forest, shimmering with untouched magic. **The gate began to hum, its silver branches curling inward like petals folding at dusk.**

For a moment, **the forest was utterly still,** as though holding its breath. **Willa stepped forward, her hand brushing the silver acorn in her pocket,** feeling the weight of everything they had worked for—the names, the stories, the magic that had been lost and found again. **This was the moment it had all been leading to.**

But just as Willa reached for the gate, **a sharp gust of wind whipped through the glade.**

The Zephyr had returned.

The wind swirled violently, snatching at the leaves in Willa's hand, tugging at the acorn in her pocket. **"You can't have it!"** Willa shouted, clutching the acorn tight. **"The forest belongs to those who believe!"**

"Words mean nothing without belief," the Zephyr hissed, twisting through the branches. **"You may have the names, but do you have the courage to carry them? The will to remember those who are gone. To weave their stories on the breeze? Are you strong enough to carry their memories and names with you forever? Most aren't, most tend to forget rather quickly to ease their own pain, to make their journey a little easier, and when they do, I am there to collect."**

Willa's heart pounded, but she stood firm. **"Yes,"** she whispered. **"I'm strong enough to remember."**

The silver acorn in her hand began to glow, warm and steady, as though it were responding to her words. **The forest had tested her—had asked her to remember, to believe, and to carry its stories.** And Willa had answered.

With a deep breath, **she placed the silver acorn into the keyhole at the center of the gate.**

The gate responded immediately. **The silver branches shimmered and twisted, opening like the petals of a flower in bloom.** The mist parted completely, revealing **a vast landscape** of snow and stars, where **the forest shimmered with untouched magic, waiting to be explored.**

Willa stepped through the gate, her heart light and full, her friends following close behind. **The forest welcomed them with open arms**, the air filled with the quiet hum of stories waiting to be told.

As the gate closed behind them, Willa knew—**the forest was whole again.** The names, the stories, the magic—they were all part of her now, woven together like threads in a tapestry. **She had found what had been lost, and in doing so, she had found herself.**

"Well done, girl," Bramble whispered, her voice warm with approval. **"The forest will never forget you."** Mr. Tawnycoat gave a pleased hum. **"Nor will we."** Larkspur buzzed happily beside her. **"See, kiddo? I told you it was worth it."**

Willa smiled, her heart full. **The journey wasn't over, but for the first time, she felt truly at home—both in the forest and in herself.**

They stood beneath the stars, **the snow-covered forest stretching out before them, filled with endless possibilities.** Willa knew that there would be more stories to tell, more adventures to come—but she wasn't afraid. Not anymore.

With the names safely carried in her heart and **the magic of the forest alive once more**, Willa stepped forward, ready for whatever lay ahead.

And the forest whispered softly around her, **"You are part of the story now."**

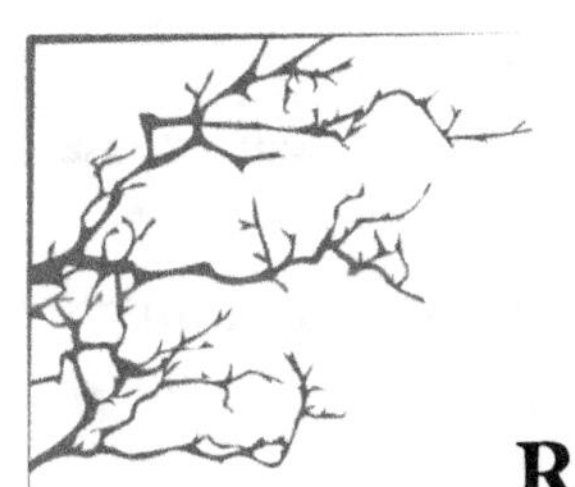

A Name Remembered

The stars glittered overhead as Willa and her companions stepped beyond the Winter Gate, **the forest unfolding around them in a vast landscape of snow-dusted branches and silvered leaves.** The air felt crisp and clean, humming with magic that had lain dormant for far too long.

Willa exhaled a cloud of white breath, **the cold wrapping around her like a soft blanket.** The ground beneath her boots crunched with frost, but instead of feeling heavy, she felt lighter—**as if the burdens she carried had been lifted.**

"This is it," Larkspur whispered, her wings glowing faintly in the starlight. **"The part where everything fits back together."**

The forest around them was no longer dark and tangled. **It felt alive again, vibrant and waiting, every branch, every leaf buzzing with quiet possibility.** And at the heart of it all, Willa could feel something stirring—**something calling to her.**

They followed the path through the snow-covered woods, **the silver branches swaying gently above them, as if welcoming them home.** At last, they came to a small glade, where **a pool of still water reflected the sky above, and a single oak tree stood, tall and proud.**

Willa approached the oak slowly, her heart racing. **The tree felt familiar, like the echo of a dream she had once known but** couldn't quite remember. At its base, nestled among the roots, was **something small and glowing—a silvered leaf, etched with her name.**

Willa knelt and picked up the leaf, her fingers brushing its smooth surface. **The letters shimmered faintly in the moonlight: Willa.**

As soon as she touched the leaf, **a wave of warmth spread through her**, and with it came a flood of memories—**her grandmother's voice, soft and steady, telling her stories beneath an old oak tree; the acorn necklace around her neck, a gift to remind her of magic; and the quiet promise her grandmother had made to her long ago.**

"You'll always belong to the forest, my little Willa," her grandmother had whispered. **"Even when you forget, the forest will remember for you."**

Tears welled in Willa's eyes as the memory settled into place, **filling the empty spaces in her heart.** She had carried the forest with her all along—**in her name, in her stories, and in the belief she had never truly lost.**

Willa stood slowly, **the silver leaf glowing softly in her hands.** She looked at Bramble, Mr. Tawnycoat, and Larkspur, her heart full. **"This is the last piece,"** she whispered. **"It was me, all along. I was part of the story."**

"Of course you were," Bramble said with a rare, gentle smile. **"The forest wouldn't be the same without you."**

"Every story needs someone to carry it," Mr. Tawnycoat added, his amber eyes twinkling. **"And you've carried this one well."**

Bramble lean in, "The names we whisper, the stories we tell—each memory is a lantern in the dark, keeping the

forgotten at bay. As long as their tales are spun through lips and minds, they linger, dancing in the quiet spaces between moments, eternal as stars. But should silence claim them—should the last story fade, the last name dissolve—the Zephyr slips in like a thief, gathering what's left, carrying them beyond even dreams. Only memory keeps the wind at bay. Never let them go."

Larkspur flitted beside her, grinning from ear to ear. "Told you, kiddo. You were the magic all along."

Willa tucked the silver leaf into her pocket, alongside the names she had found: **Elspeth, Rowan, Elowen. Each name, each story, was part of the forest—but they were also part of her.** And now that she had remembered, the magic was whole again.

As Willa stood beneath the oak tree, **the forest around her began to bloom.** Leaves unfurled along the branches, shimmering with silver and gold. **Flowers sprang from the snow**, glowing softly in the moonlight, their petals swirling with colors too beautiful to describe. **The air shimmered with magic**, and the hum of stories filled the clearing, like the gentle strumming of a harp.

"**It's beautiful**," Willa whispered, turning in place to take it all in. "**The forest remembers**," Bramble said softly, her eyes bright. "**And it will never forget again.**"

Willa took a deep breath, **the cold air filling her lungs with hope.** The forest had given her something she hadn't known she needed—**a place to belong, a story to carry, and the belief that magic was never truly lost.**

She knelt once more at the base of the oak tree and placed **the silver acorn among its roots. It glimmered softly, settling into place like it had always belonged there.**

"I'll keep believing," Willa whispered, brushing her fingers gently over the roots. **"I'll carry these stories with me, no matter where I go."**

The oak tree seemed to sigh in contentment, its branches swaying gently in the night air. As the first hints of dawn brightened the horizon, Willa knew it was time to leave. **The forest would always be a part of her now—but she also knew she needed to carry its magic back to the world outside.**

"Time to go, kid," Larkspur said softly, perching on Willa's shoulder. **"The magic won't do any good if you keep it all to yourself."**

Mr. Tawnycoat gave a slow, solemn nod. **"The forest will always be here when you need it. But now it's time to live your story out there."**

Bramble adjusted her shawl and gave Willa an approving look. **"You've done well, girl. Don't forget what you've learned here."**

Willa smiled, her heart full. **"I won't."** With one last glance at the oak tree and the glowing forest around her, **Willa stepped back onto the path, her companions at her side.** They walked together toward the edge of the forest, **the silvered leaves whispering goodbye as they passed.**

And as the Winter Gate shimmered behind them, closing softly like the last page of a book, Willa knew that **the magic wasn't gone. It never would be.**

When Willa reached the edge of the forest, **the sun was rising,** casting the world in shades of gold and pink. The air smelled of pine and snow, and **the acorn necklace around her neck felt warm, like a quiet promise kept.**

She knew the magic would follow her, no matter where she went. And though the forest might fade into the background of her everyday life, **it would always be there, waiting—just beneath the surface of the world, ready to be found again.** Larkspur buzzed beside her, grinning. **"So... what now, kiddo?"**

Willa smiled, adjusting her scarf against the cold. **"Now? Now we tell the stories."** And with that, **she stepped forward into the morning, ready to carry the magic wherever it was needed most.**

Epilogue – The Garden Waits

Somewhere deep within the forest, beneath a canopy of silvered leaves and golden light, **the Garden of Forgotten Names bloomed once more.** The air shimmered with magic, and the soft hum of stories filled every branch and root. **Each leaf that drifted to the ground whispered a name—some old, some new, all remembered.**

The garden would wait, as it always had, for those who needed it most: **the lost, the wanderers, the dreamers who still believed in magic, even when the world tried to make them forget.**

Months had passed since Willa left the forest, but **its magic stayed with her.** It was in the way she saw the world differently now—**the way she noticed the little things: the shape of a leaf, the hum of the wind, the feeling of belonging tucked into the corners of a quiet afternoon.** The forest hadn't disappeared—it was still with her, **woven into her heart like the names she carried.**

At home, **the acorn necklace hung from her bedpost, a constant reminder of the journey she had taken.** And sometimes, when she touched it, she swore she could still hear **the soft rustling of the forest, whispering stories just for her.**

Willa had started to tell stories—little ones at first, shared with friends at school or whispered to herself at night. **They were simple tales: about foxes with lanterns, fairies with mischief in their hearts, and witches who lived in treehouses and made the best hazelnut tea.** But every time she told one, she felt the magic stir, a reminder that **stories had power.**

She knew now that **every story—whether big or small—mattered.** Because stories were what kept magic alive, what connected people and places, what carried hope through the darkest winters.

And so Willa told her stories, **believing that each word she spoke was a seed planted in the hearts of those who listened, ready to bloom when the time was right.**

Far away, in the heart of the forest, **the Garden of Forgotten Names waited patiently beneath its golden canopy.** It didn't mind waiting—**it had waited before and would wait again**—because it knew that eventually, someone would find their way back. **A child who had lost something precious, a dreamer seeking answers, or a wanderer who needed to remember who they truly were.**

And when they did, **the garden would be ready.** It would bloom beneath the light of the stars, **its leaves whispering names like promises: Elspeth, Rowan, Elowen—and Willa.**

Because some things are never truly lost. **They are simply waiting to be found again.**

On a quiet autumn afternoon, Willa stood beneath the old oak tree in the park near her house. **The air smelled of apples and woodsmoke**, and the leaves drifted lazily from the branches, swirling in the breeze. **Willa closed her eyes, breathing in the scent of the season.**

She reached into her pocket and pulled out **a small silver leaf—the one the forest had given her, etched with her name.** She smiled, her heart full, and with a quiet whisper, she let it fall gently to the ground.

The wind carried it away, and as it drifted through the air, Willa knew that **the forest had not forgotten her—and it never would.**

A Story That Never Ends

And so the garden waits, the stories linger, and the forest hums with quiet magic, ready to be found by those who believe. **Because magic—true magic—is never truly gone.**

It lives in the stories we tell, **the names we remember, and the quiet moments when we believe in something bigger than ourselves.**

And if you listen closely—**on a crisp autumn night, beneath the rustling leaves—you might just hear the forest calling your name, waiting to welcome you home.**

www.ingramcontent.com/pod-product-compliance
Lightning Source LLC
Chambersburg PA
CBHW051352150726

48000CB00003B/1147